Hello Baby

Jenni Overend

Julie Vivas

FRANCES LINCOLN CHILDREN'S BOOKS

We've been waiting a long time for this day, Mum, Dad, Bea, Janie and me. Mum's got pains in her tummy and that means her baby is ready to be born.

Bea and Janie are making a giant bed by the fire for Mum and the baby.

I help Mum put the baby's clothes out
onto the table. The socks are tiny enough
to fit on my thumbs.

'Tonight we'll be dressing the baby in its
new clothes, Jack,' Mum says to me.

It's hard to imagine.

I wonder if it's a boy or a girl.

I would like a brother.

Bobbo is barking. That must be the midwife, Anna, arriving.

It's wild outside. There's a roaring wind and the clouds are racing madly. I feel like racing too.

'I'm going for a walk in the wild wind,' says Mum. 'It'll help the baby along.'

I think if I was a baby listening to that wind, I'd want to stay inside Mum, floating in the warm water.

Anna is spreading all her things
out on the table.
    There's a special microphone
for listening to the baby's heart,
and oxygen in case the baby needs it.

Janie is talking to Nan on the phone, telling her
that Mum is fine.

'We'll need to bring in some more wood, Jack,' Dad says.
'The room has to be really warm for a new baby.'

Our neighbour, Harry, dropped us off a load of wood last
week. He said it was a present for the baby. I thought it was a
strange present then, but I don't now.

Mum's back at last.

I tell Dad I think Mum should sit down and rest, but he says she will probably keep walking. And she does — round and round the living room. She stops every now and then and leans on Dad.

Auntie Meg, Mum's sister, arrives. She has a pot of soup and a bunch of yellow and orange poppies. She puts the soup by the fire and sits next to me, holding my hand.

'When will the baby come?' I ask her.

'Soon,' she says.

Bea and Janie both saw me being born, but I've never seen anyone born.

Mum has told me that she might make a lot of noise but I mustn't worry because that's what it's like when babies are born. She'll feel better if she yells and screams.

Mum's stopped walking now and is leaning
on Dad by the fire, rocking from side to side.
And she's right — every few minutes she yells
so loudly the whole town will know we're
having our baby today!

Just then the phone rings. I answer it, but
I can't hear who it is because Mum is still yelling.

I yell, 'Mum's having a baby!' as loudly as I can,
and I feel much better. The person hangs up.
I would too, if I heard that noise on the other end
of the phone.

Auntie Meg is calling me: 'Quick, quick, the
baby's head is coming!'

I kneel down near Mum and see a round black shape between her legs.

Mum's pushing and yelling.

Suddenly there's a little, red scrunched-up face! I'm twisting Bea's jumper into a knot. She doesn't notice. She's got tears running down her face, but she doesn't wipe them off.

Janie is looking a bit white, and Dad can't see the baby because he's supporting Mum.

I watch as Anna holds the baby's head, helping it out.

The baby slips into Anna's hands,
and she lifts the cord from around the
baby's neck, and I can see it's a boy!
And then I hear a little sound,
like a kitten meowing.
'Hello, baby,' I say quietly. 'Hello.'

Dad is helping Mum onto the bed.
She is shaking. Dad wraps her up.

Mum lies against the cushions.

'A little boy,' Mum says, crying and smiling
at the same time. She holds him close against
her breast. Dad tucks the blanket around them.
He's crying too.

Anna gently pulls on the cord between Mum's legs and out comes a big purple and red shape.

'The placenta,' says Anna. She lays it out on a dish and looks at it carefully.

'Beautiful,' she says. 'A very healthy placenta. Lucky baby.'

'You can cut the cord now,' Anna says to Dad. He uses special strong scissors.

Mum is leaning back, watching our new baby.

'What do you think?' she says.

'Great,' I say.

Anna gently takes the baby down by the fire and dresses him.
The tiny clothes look too big.

It is very dark now and the wind has dropped. Auntie Meg
kisses Mum, and leaves. Anna gathers up all her things and
hugs Mum. 'I'll be back tomorrow,' she says.

Dad gets more firewood and makes us toast and soup.

He puts on some music.

I eat in bed with Mum. She isn't hungry, but she needs a drink.

'Thirsty work, having babies,' she says to me.

Janie's getting our sleeping-bags. We're all sleeping by the fire tonight.

The music finishes. The only sound is the fire. Dad lights a night-light
on the wall.

I lie for a long time in my sleeping-bag, watching the
fire make patterns on everyone's faces.

Slowly we all stop talking. I can see the baby's head on
Mum's shoulder. He's between Mum and Dad which is
where I'd like to be.

I sneak out of my bag and hop in next to Dad.
It's warm. He cuddles me in. I bet the baby's warm too.
'Good night, baby,' I say. 'This is your first night
in the world. Good night.'

To those who inspired, encouraged,
supported and loved — thank you.
J.O.

To Alison and Betty.
J.V.

Text copyright © Jenni Overend 1999
Illustrations copyright © Julie Vivas 1999

This edition published in 2004
by Frances Lincoln Children's Books,
4 Torriano Mews, Torriano Ave, London NW5 2RZ

www.franceslincoln.com

First published in 1999 by ABC Books,
for the Australian Broadcasting Corporation

British Library Cataloguing in Publication Data
available on request

ISBN 1-84507-023-2 (hardback)
ISBN 1-84507-110-7 (paperback)

Printed in the UK